BATMAN
THE BRAVE AND THE BOLD

THE EYES OF DESPERO!

adapted by Jake Black
based on the teleplay by J.M. DeMatteis
Batman created by Bob Kane

cover illustration by Dan Panosian

Grosset & Dunlap
An Imprint of Penguin Group (USA) Inc.

GROSSET & DUNLAP
Published by the Penguin Group
Penguin Group (USA) Inc., 375 Hudson Street, New York, New York 10014, USA
Penguin Group (Canada), 90 Eglinton Avenue East, Suite 700,
Toronto, Ontario M4P 2Y3, Canada
(a division of Pearson Penguin Canada Inc.)
Penguin Books Ltd., 80 Strand, London WC2R ORL, England
Penguin Group Ireland, 25 St. Stephen's Green, Dublin 2, Ireland
(a division of Penguin Books Ltd.)
Penguin Group (Australia), 250 Camberwell Road, Camberwell, Victoria 3124, Australia
(a division of Pearson Australia Group Pty. Ltd.)
Penguin Books India Pvt. Ltd., 11 Community Centre, Panchsheel Park,
New Delhi–110 017, India
Penguin Group (NZ), 67 Apollo Drive, Rosedale, North Shore 0632, New Zealand
(a division of Pearson New Zealand Ltd.)
Penguin Books (South Africa) (Pty.) Ltd., 24 Sturdee Avenue,
Rosebank, Johannesburg 2196, South Africa

Penguin Books Ltd., Registered Offices:
80 Strand, London WC2R ORL, England

The publisher does not have any control over and does not assume any responsibility for author or third-party websites or their content.

Library of Congress Cataloging-in-Publication Data

Black, Jake.
The eyes of Despero! / adapted by Jake Black.
p. cm.
Based on the television program "Batman: The Brave and the Bold."
ISBN 978-0-448-45385-9 (pbk.)
I. Batman, the brave and the bold (Television program) II. Title.
PZ7.B52893Ey 2010
[E]--dc22
2009025335

ISBN 978-0-448-45385-9   10 9 8 7 6 5 4 3 2 1

CHAPTER 1

For thousands of years, the Green Lantern Corps has protected the galaxy from numerous threats. Based on the planet Oa, the Green Lanterns are led by a mysterious group of governors known as the Guardians. The Guardians have always lived in peace on Oa. Therefore, it was a great surprise when Despero, a three-eyed villain, chose to attack Oa and the

Green Lantern Corps. The Guardians dispatched many of the Green Lanterns into space to confront Despero.

High above the planet Oa, the Green Lantern Corps, led by the greatest Green Lantern of all—Hal Jordan—stared down Despero.

"So, this is the legendary Green Lantern Corps. How pathetic," Despero said in disgust.

Hal Jordan glared back at the would-be ruler of the galaxy. "What's pathetic, Despero, is a tyrant like you thinking you can turn the Green Lantern Corps into your own personal army."

Hal and the Green Lanterns charged toward Despero with great speed. However, they were no match for Despero. He blasted a powerful pink ray from his third eye. The ray covered most

of the Green Lanterns. The Green Lanterns, except for Hal Jordan, were now under Despero's control.

Despero laughed in victory. "I have the power to bend the Green Lanterns' will to mine! And your masters, the Guardians of the Universe, will be next."

Hal Jordan pointed his ring at Despero, ready

to fight. "The Guardians have been moved to a safe place."

Hal Jordan fired off green missiles from his power ring. The missiles sailed toward Despero. But Despero hid behind the other Green Lanterns. Together, they blocked Hal's missiles.

"Submit to me willingly, Jordan, and together we'll bring forth a golden age unlike any ever seen before," Despero said.

Hal glared hard at Despero. "You mean an age of servitude where every individual is just an extension of your mind? No, thanks."

Hal extended his ring hand outward and spoke the Green Lantern oath: "In brightest day, in blackest night, no evil shall escape my sight. Let those who worship evil's might beware my power . . . Green Lantern's light!"

From his power ring, a massive surge of green energy flashed forward. Despero shielded his three eyes. The powerful energy passed over the Green Lanterns who were under Despero's control.

Soon the light faded and Despero opened his eyes. He was all alone. Hal Jordan and the other Green Lanterns were gone. Despero looked around in surprise.

"So, Jordan chose to destroy himself and the corps—rather than leave them in my power. A minor annoyance . . . requiring a minor change in plans," Despero said as he flew away.

Unnoticed by Despero, Hal Jordan's power ring raced through space away from Oa as well. The ring was headed for Earth.

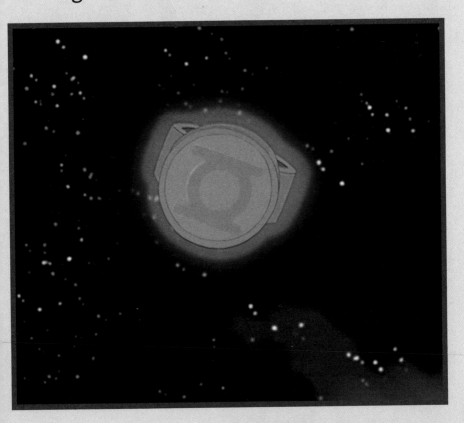

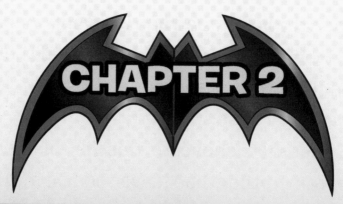

CHAPTER 2

It was a typical day in Gotham City. The alarm at the Gotham First National Bank sounded. Once again, it was being robbed by a crook who thought he could get away with it. But, as usual, the Caped Crusader stood in his way. This time, it was Cavalier, an old, English-speaking foe who found fighting Batman to be great sport.

Cavalier shimmied down a drainpipe on the side of the bank building, carrying sacks of cash. At the bottom of the pipe was Batman, waiting for the musketeer-like menace.

"Batman! If thou thinkest thou canst stop me—then have thee!" Cavalier yelled as he drew his sword.

Batman grabbed a garbage can lid as a shield, and whispered, "Somewhere, Shakespeare is spinning in his grave."

Cavalier thrust his sword toward Batman, calling out, "Thou art no match for the Cavalier! Witty rogue! Daring thief!"

Batman grew a little annoyed with the Cavalier's ego. "Delusional loon?" he asked, mocking Cavalier.

The Caped Crusader grabbed Cavalier's sword, and used it against the thief himself. Batman hit Cavalier on the head with the hilt of the sword, knocking him unconscious. Cavalier slumped to the ground, defeated.

Batman heard a pair of police sirens racing toward the bank and turned to the sound. Just then, Batman saw a Green Lantern power ring floating toward him! Batman reached out his hand to grab the ring.

A Green Lantern power ring? Batman thought to himself.

Suddenly, a green bubble burst from the ring, surrounding Batman. The police cars arrived.

But Batman didn't see the arrest. He was being carried up into outer space by a huge, green bubble. The bubble opened a portal in space, carrying Batman through it. The hole then closed up, and Batman and the green bubble disappeared!

CHAPTER 3

At the center of the universe, in the space above the planet Oa, another space portal opened. The glowing, green sphere carrying Batman raced toward the planet below. The sphere landed softly in the center of a large building complex on Oa.

"Oa, Green Lantern headquarters," Batman said, looking around.

The massive building appeared abandoned. Where had all the Green Lanterns gone, Batman wondered. Batman wandered through the hallways.

Suddenly, a short distance away, he heard a strange, howling noise. It was as if an animal was hurt or scared. Batman ran as fast as he could toward the noise.

The howl seemed to be coming from under a metal grate on the floor. Batman lifted the grate and jumped down into a hole. As he got close to the howl, Batman heard another sound: voices.

"Shut yer furry yap, will ya?" one of the voices snapped.

"But I'm singing," said the howler.

Batman recognized the speakers. The first was Guy Gardner, one of the Green Lanterns assigned to protect Earth. The other was G'nort, a doglike Green Lantern.

The Caped Crusader saw that Gardner and G'nort were being held behind bars in the Green Lantern jail. He called out Gardner's name.

"What are *you* doing here?" Gardner asked.

Batman smirked back at Gardner as he opened the cell door. "Apparently rescuing you," Batman said.

Batman stepped into the cell and the Green Lantern ring floated just above his shoulder.

"Hey! That ring is GL Corps property, and you ain't GL Corps!" Gardner snapped.

Another Green Lantern stepped from the shadows near Batman and Gardner.

"Back away, Gardner. Now," the mysterious Green Lantern warned. "I'm Sinestro, Green Lantern of Space Sector 1417. Which has the lowest crime rate in the known galaxy."

Batman looked at the three captured Green Lanterns curiously. "Why are you three locked up in the brig here?"

Sinestro explained that, earlier that morning, Gardner had a little tantrum when the cafeteria cook served him poached eggs instead of scrambled. Sinestro, meanwhile, had been protecting a peaceful world from the Warlords of Okaara, and had attacked the warlords after they had surrendered.

"The warlords are well-known for striking once their opponent's guard is down," Sinestro explained. "Sometimes we have to bend the rules to protect the innocent. I'm sure you understand."

Batman turned his attention to G'nort. The humanoid dog saluted Batman as he explained his story.

"G'nort Esplanade G'neesmacher—Green Lantern of Space Sector X-minus 5267.2. I was bringing the prisoners lunch, and accidentally locked myself in," G'nort said, embarrassed.

Batman motioned for Sinestro, Gardner, and G'nort to follow him out of the brig.

"Whatever the reason, being in here saved you from the fate that befell the other Green Lanterns," Batman said grimly.

CHAPTER 4

Moments later, Batman, Sinestro, G'nort, and Gardner stood in the central command room of the Green Lantern headquarters. A massive energy battery, used to power the Green Lantern Corps' rings, surged behind them.

Hal Jordan's power ring lit up in a vivid display. As though it were a movie projector, the ring showed the battle with Despero and the disappearance of the Green Lantern Corps.

"Despero, the most dangerous humanoid in the galaxy," Sinestro said.

Gardner turned to Batman and said dismissively, "Thanks for stopping by, Bats. Looks like we've got some work to do."

Batman shook his head. "Jordan's ring came to me for a reason, and I get the feeling that I'm going to need more than a Batarang against this guy."

Gardner's face grew hard. G'nort looked worried. It was Green Lantern Corps policy that only a member of the corps could use a power ring. Sinestro moved close to Batman.

"We can use our rings to augment you," Sinestro said, pointing his ring at Batman.

Gardner and G'nort stood next to Sinestro. Together, they repeated the Green Lantern oath.

Streams of bright green energy blasted out of the three rings. The waves washed over Batman, covering him in an emerald glow. Quickly, the light faded, revealing Batman now dressed in green armor.

"I don't suppose it comes in blue," Batman joked.

Sinestro shook his head and said, "Remember, your power suit will respond to your will, much as our rings do."

Batman looked down at his suit and smiled confidently. "Let's go!" he said.

With that, Batman, Sinestro, Gardner, and G'nort soared into space, searching for Despero and the missing Green Lanterns.

CHAPTER 5

Batman and his Green Lantern allies were investigating the scene of the other Green Lanterns' disappearance. Batman asked the small band of heroes to move faster.

"What a minute, who put *you* in charge?" Gardner demanded.

"I did," Batman simply said. "The freedom of the entire universe is on the line, and our first

duty is to the innocent people we've sworn to protect and serve," Batman argued. "The more we fight, the farther away Despero gets."

"I'm closer than you think," Despero boomed as he appeared in front of Batman and the three Green Lanterns. This time, he was fifty times larger than before.

"Wowzer! That boy's had a real growth spurt!" G'nort said.

The third eye on Despero's face glowed

bright red. Despero declared that he would take control of the universe with the power of his advanced mind. Batman pointed toward Despero, and ordered Gardner and G'nort to take the left flank.

"Eat my toenail clippings," Gardner said dismissively, and flew ahead to fight Despero on his own.

G'nort saluted the heroic leader and said, "Don't worry, Mr. Batman, sir, I'll take the left flank. But, um, which way is left?"

Gardner slammed into Despero's eye. In an explosion of red energy, Gardner was blasted backward past Batman, Sinestro, and G'nort. The three remaining heroes lined up and pointed their powerful emerald weapons at Despero.

"Fire," Batman said.

Streams of green energy shot from Batman's armor and Sinestro's ring. G'nort's ring sputtered, unable to blast any sort of energy.

"I knew I should have charged this sucker," G'nort said.

As Batman and Sinestro continued to battle Despero, the villain's third eye fired back. Despero hit the three Green Lanterns and Batman with a blast of energy that tied each hero up in unbreakable golden energy bands!

CHAPTER 6

Batman, Sinestro, Gardner, and G'nort were trapped in Despero's energy bands. Frozen, they were unable to fight back. Sinestro floated near Batman and whispered a message to the Caped Crusader.

"Your armor and my ring are all about using your will. Focus that and there's no limit to what I . . . we . . . can do," Sinestro said.

Batman took Sinestro's advice, and by force of will was able to break free of the golden energy bands. Despero grew angry as the heroes freed themselves. He blasted another stream of energy from his third eye. Acting quickly, Batman and Sinestro fired back, forming a green sphere around Despero. The sphere caught Despero's energy blast, turning it back on him. In a massive explosion, Despero disappeared.

Sinestro grew concerned. "It was all an illusion," he said.

"Why should I be there when my mind is

powerful enough to do the work for me?"
Despero's voice boomed out. "I draw closer
to my goal: the Green Lantern that will be my
ultimate weapon!"

Batman was confused. "I thought you three
were the only Green Lanterns left?"

"Hokey smokes! He's going after Mogo!"
G'nort said, terrified.

Mogo was a living planet who was also a Green Lantern. Billions of people lived on Mogo's surface.

Despero floated high above the planet Mogo. Focusing his third eye, he blasted a shot of energy that covered the entire planet.

"Now to remake Mogo in my own image!" Despero screamed.

The citizens of Mogo fell under Despero's will. The biggest, most powerful Green Lantern was now a great weapon to be used at the hands of Despero.

"Now that Mogo's power is mine, I will move on to my next target: Earth—home to Hal Jordan, Guy Gardner, Batman, and a vast array of superpowered beings that I can bend to my will!" Despero called out.

Batman, G'nort, Gardner, and Sinestro heard Despero's threat from across the galaxy. Together, they raced through the vastness of space, desperate to stop the villain from achieving his evil goals.

CHAPTER 7

As Mogo and Despero moved closer to Earth, Batman stood with G'nort, Sinestro, and Gardner on a nearby asteroid, preparing their attack. Batman had a plan to free Mogo from Despero's control.

"Our only hope is to drain Mogo's Green Lantern power into one of your rings," Batman said.

"Take the weapon out of Despero's hands," Sinestro said, understanding what Batman had in mind.

Batman ordered Sinestro to fly ahead of Mogo and the team and use his power ring to place a protective shield around Earth. Without questioning the leader, Sinestro took off from the asteroid, his mission firmly in mind.

Batman turned to Gardner and said, "I'll keep Despero busy. Gardner, you do the same with Mogo."

Gardner opened his mouth to protest, but thought better of it. He understood that Batman knew what he was doing. After all, it was Earth, Gardner's home planet, that was at risk. Igniting his ring, Gardner set out to confront Mogo.

Batman turned to face G'nort. The doglike Green Lantern secretly hoped his job would be to guard the asteroid, but Batman had more important things in mind. G'nort would drain Mogo's power battery into his own ring.

"I don't know if I can do this, Mr. Batman, sir. Everybody knows I'm just a screwup. Maybe somebody else better do it. My

ringy-ding ain't got much power left, and—"
G'nort stammered.

Batman looked at G'nort very seriously.
"There isn't anyone else, G'nort. Just remember,
it's not the ring . . . it's the man."

G'nort smiled nervously, and said, "I'm not
exactly a man, but if a guy like you's got faith in
me, then I'll give it my best shot!"

Batman nodded. He and G'nort leaped from the asteroid into space. The two heroes parted ways, focused on their respective tasks.

Batman didn't get very far, however. Despero appeared directly in front of Batman's path. From his third eye, Despero once again ensnared Batman in golden bands of energy.

"There's no way you can defeat me," Despero said. "Gardner's a loose cannon. The dog is an idiot. And Sinestro, well, would you like to hear the full story of Sinestro's imprisonment? I learned it when I scanned his mind."

Batman floated silently in space as Despero told the dark tale of Sinestro; the powerful

Green Lantern had not only attacked warlords after they'd surrendered, but he destroyed every living being on their ships. Then he set up a puppet government—loyal only to him—on the very planet he'd sworn to protect.

"Sinestro and I both seek to impose order on a chaotic universe," Despero said. "He will be a wonderful soldier in my cause. As will you."

Meanwhile, Gardner landed on Mogo's surface, planning to distract the living planet. He was shocked to see that Sinestro was also there, setting up massive bombs.

"What are you doing here? You're supposed

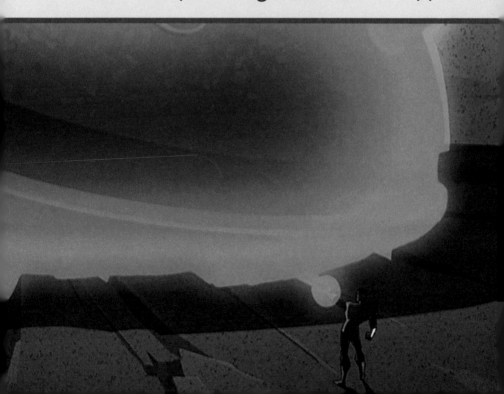

to be protecting Earth!" Gardner demanded angrily.

"That's what I'm doing," Sinestro said darkly. "I can't leave Earth in your hands or G'nort's, so I'm going to blow Mogo to bits."

Gardner ignited his ring and warned Sinestro, "I can't let you do that. Mogo's a living being."

Deep in the center of the planet Mogo, G'nort stood in front of a giant Green Lantern power battery. G'nort nervously raised his ring.

"Okay, all I gotta do is say the oath and save the world. I'll never get this. I can't remember it! . . . In sunniest day, in cloudiest night . . . no!

That's not it!" G'nort slapped himself, trying to remember. "On Labor Day, on Halloween night, no nose hair shall escape my sight!"

G'nort looked at the ground sadly. "It's hopeless."

CHAPTER 8

Gardner knew that he had to stop Sinestro from destroying Mogo. The two Green Lanterns fought, using their power rings to create weapons to use against each other. Sinestro had turned his back on what the Green Lantern Corps stood for. Although Gardner sometimes thought he was a better hero than the other Green Lanterns, he knew that being part of the team was more important. He had to stop Sinestro!

High above Mogo, Batman focused his will and once again freed himself from Despero's bands. With twin blasts of green energy, Batman fought against Despero, buying G'nort more time.

Deep inside Mogo, at the power battery, G'nort remembered that he had written the Green Lantern oath on his wrist. Looking at his wrist, he read aloud, "In brightest day, in blackest night, no evil shall escape my sight. Let those who worship evil's might beware my power . . . Green Lantern's light!"

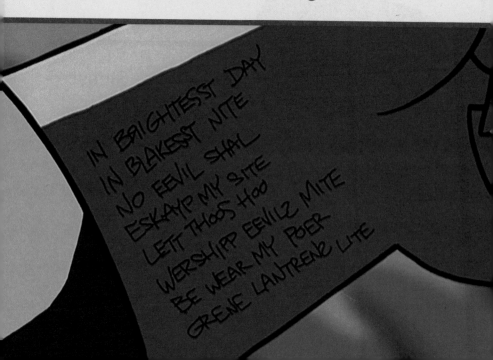

Mogo's power battery surged in a bright green display. The energy flowed into G'nort's ring. He helped save the day!

On the surface of Mogo, Sinestro and Gardner continued to fight, but Gardner was able to bite Sinestro's hand, throwing him off Mogo and winning the battle.

"You didn't think I was above fighting dirty, did ya?" Gardner said to Sinestro.

Batman wrestled with Despero in space, but Despero had grown weaker. Now free from Despero's power, Mogo blasted several giant rocks from his surface into space, slamming them into Despero.

"Thanks, Mogo," Batman said.

Despero was defeated, Sinestro's dark plans were stopped, and G'nort helped save the day.

Hal Jordan's ring floated out of Batman's utility belt. In a splash of emerald energy, Hal Jordan and the entire Green Lantern Corps materialized in front of Batman.

"You were all in the ring?" Batman asked.

"I sent it to you for safekeeping. I had a hunch you'd be able to get us out of this mess." Hal smiled, putting his ring back on his hand.

Later, in the cafeteria on Oa, Gardner, Batman, G'nort, and the Green Lantern Corps celebrated their victory over Despero.

"If it wasn't for me, Earth woulda been kaput. The whole universe woulda been toast," Gardner boasted.

"Gardner!" Batman called to Guy. All of the Lanterns turned to see what Batman had to say. "Good job, Guy," Batman said. "So what did you end up doing with Sinestro?"

"Oh, don't worry about him," Gardner said, pointing to his ring. "He's in a safe place. Hate to say it, but you made a pretty good Lantern out there."

"Thanks," Batman said. "But if there's one Lantern here who deserves the credit, it's G'nort."

G'nort rushed into Batman's arms and gave him a big lick across the face. "G'nort, I told you, no licking."

Then Batman turned to face Guy. "He's the true hero, Gardner," Batman said. "Remember, it's not the ring, but the man—or dog—that uses it."

G'nort blushed, embarrassed at being the hero.

Everybody was happy—the Green Lantern Corps saved the galaxy. With a little help from Batman, of course.